A Cinderella glass slippers?

"I think we're rehearsing the ballroom scene," Nancy called out to her friends.

"I *love* that scene," Bess gushed. "It's so pretty!"

They got to the top of the stairs. Nancy expected to see all the students stretching at the barre and on the floor. But instead, everyone was huddled around Mr. McGuire. He looked very serious.

Andrea turned around and saw Nancy and her friends. She came running up to them. "Nancy! Bess! George!" she cried out. Her eyes were shiny with tears.

"Andrea, what's going on?" Nancy asked her curiously.

"My Cinderella slippers are gone," Andrea announced. "Somebody stole them!"

Join the CLUE CREW
& solve these other cases!

NANCY DREW
AND THE CLUE CREW

#4

The Cinderella Ballet Mystery

BY CAROLYN KEENE

ILLUSTRATED BY MACKY PAMINTUAN

Aladdin

New York   London   Toronto   Sydney   New Delhi

This book is a work of fiction. Any references to historical events, real people, or real locales are used fictitiously. Other names, characters, places, and incidents are the product of the author's imagination, and any resemblance to actual events or locales or persons, living or dead, is entirely coincidental.

 ALADDIN

An imprint of Simon & Schuster Children's Publishing Division

1230 Avenue of the Americas, New York, NY 10020

This Aladdin paperback edition July 2022

Text copyright © 2006 by Simon & Schuster, Inc.

Illustrations copyright © 2006 by Macky Pamintuan

All rights reserved, including the right of reproduction in whole or in part in any form.

ALADDIN and related logo, NANCY DREW, and NANCY DREW AND THE CLUE CREW are registered trademarks of Simon & Schuster, Inc. For information about special discounts for bulk purchases, please contact Simon & Schuster Special Sales at 1-866-506-1949 or business@simonandschuster.com.

The Simon & Schuster Speakers Bureau can bring authors to your live event.

For more information or to book an event contact the Simon & Schuster Speakers Bureau at 1-866-248-3049 or visit our website at www.simonspeakers.com.

Designed by Lisa Vega

The text of this book was set in ITC Stone Informal.

Manufactured in the United States of America 0223 NGS

10 9 8 7 6 5

Library of Congress Control Number 2006920995

ISBN 978-1-6659-3088-8

CONTENTS

CHAPTER ONE

The Cinderella Ballet

Nancy Drew slipped on her pink ballet shoes. "Let's stretch!" she said to her friends George Fayne and Bess Marvin.

George nodded. "Last one to the barre is a rotten egg!"

"Hey, not fair, you're closest to the barre!" Bess cried out.

The three friends hurried to the long wooden bar in front of the mirrored wall. Running was against the rules at Tim McGuire's Dance Studio, so they walked really, really fast instead.

The three girls had been taking lessons at Mr. McGuire's studio since the beginning of the school year. They were in the middle of rehearsing for a full-length ballet of "Cinderella." Opening night was on Saturday, only five days away.

Nancy got to the barre first, then Bess, then George. "Hmm, I wonder who's the rotten egg?" Bess joked.

George made a face. "Ha, ha."

Nancy put her right foot up on the barre with her toes pointed. She held onto the barre for balance. Then she curved her left arm over her head and leaned her body toward her right foot. Bess and George did the same. Nancy could feel the muscles in her right leg and the whole left side of her body stretching and getting loose.

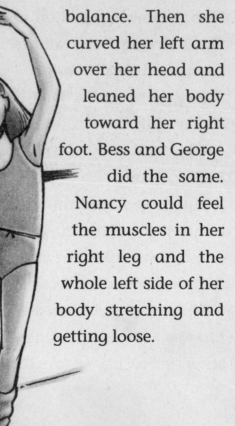

Nancy glanced at the wall clock; it was five minutes before four. *Almost time for the rehearsal to begin,* she thought. The studio was filled with students who were busily putting on their ballet slippers or stretching.

Nancy noticed that Mr. McGuire was off in the corner talking on his tiny silver cell phone. His eyebrows were knit tightly together, and his mouth was pursed in a deep frown. Nancy thought that he looked upset. She wondered who he was talking to.

"Hey, Nancy Drew! I have a mystery for you," someone said.

Nancy glanced over her shoulder. Deirdre Shannon was standing there. Deirdre's best friend, Madison Foley, was standing next to her. They were dressed in identical shiny, purple leotards with matching supershort shorts, pink tights, and pink leg warmers.

"It's the mystery of the weird ballet outfit," Deirdre continued. "Did aliens come and dress

George Fayne in the middle of the night? Curious minds want to know!"

George was wearing a soccer T-shirt and shorts instead of a fancy leotard combo like Deirdre. Mr. McGuire didn't have strict rules about what to wear for rehearsals.

"You're so hilarious, Deirdre," George said. "Not!"

Deirdre cracked up. She looked over at Madison, who was searching through her dance bag for something, and poked her with an elbow.

"What? Oh!" Madison started cracking up too. Madison always did whatever Deirdre told her to do.

Nancy rolled her eyes and resumed stretching. She and her friends were used to getting all kinds of attention, even teasing, about the Clue Crew.

The Clue Crew was Nancy, Bess, and George's mystery-solving club. Their headquarters were located in Nancy's room. They stored their clues in one of Nancy's desk drawers. George kept track of their cases on Nancy's computer.

Just then, a boy named Gregory Auffredou came up to the girls. He was wearing a black T-shirt with the words "Dancing Fool" on it, black sweat pants, and black ballet shoes. He gave a friendly wave.

"Hi," Gregory said. "My mom made some chocolate chip cookies. Does anyone want one?" He reached into his dance bag and pulled out a plastic container.

"Yum! Thanks!" Bess plucked a cookie out of the container and bit into it. She began coughing and gagging. "Yuck! What is this?"

Gregory burst into laughter. "I got you!" he guffawed. "These cookies are totally fake. They're from my sister's toy kitchen."

Deirdre quickly took her digital camera out of her dance bag and snapped a picture. "I got you too Bess!" she giggled.

She held out the tiny screen on her camera for everyone to see. She had managed to get a picture of Bess's grossed-out expression and

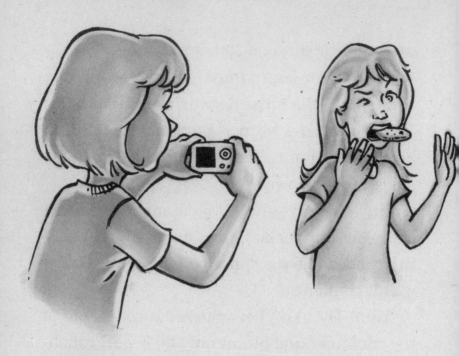

the fake cookie hanging out of her mouth.

Nancy shook her head at Gregory. He always seemed to be playing practical jokes. Once he'd put fake worms in George's water bottle. Another time he'd put ice cubes in Madison's ballet slippers.

Bess handed the "cookie" back to Gregory. "You can have this back," she said huffily. She turned to Deirdre. "And you can delete that picture!"

"No way," Deirdre said with a grin. "I might

even post it on my website!" Deirdre had her own website, called Dishing with Deirdre. Her father had helped her set it up.

"Don't you dare!" Bess cried out.

Mr. McGuire clapped his hands. "Girls and boys! I want everyone on the floor. Now."

Nancy and her friends hurried over to the middle of the floor and sat down with their legs crossed. Deirdre, Madison, and Gregory sat down nearby.

The other students in the class included Nadine Nardo and Andrea Wu from River Heights Elementary School. There were also about a dozen kids who went to other schools. In "Cinderella," Gregory played the part of the prince. Deirdre and Madison were the wicked stepsisters. George was the wicked stepmother. Bess was the fairy godmother. Nancy, Nadine, and Andrea were mice who magically turned into Cinderella's coach drivers. They were also dancers and attendants at the prince's ball, along with some other kids.

The lead role of Cinderella was played by a girl named Autumn Gooden. Nancy glanced around. Autumn wasn't here yet. It wasn't like her to be late for class.

Scruffy, Mr. McGuire's golden retriever, came up to Gregory and gave him a kiss. For some reason, Scruffy loved to give Gregory wet, sloppy dog kisses. Nancy wondered if it was because Gregory often fed the dog cookies—*real* cookies—when Mr. McGuire wasn't looking!

Mr. McGuire sat down on his special blue director's chair in the front of the studio. "Hello, class," he began.

"Hi, Mr. McGuire," the class replied in unison.

Mr. McGuire had light brown hair and a slender, serious face. He used to be a professional ballet dancer. Nancy, George, and Bess had seen him in a production of *The Nutcracker* last year in Chicago. Nancy had loved the special holiday ballet, especially the second act, which was set entirely in the Land of Sweets. The stage had been filled with giant-size candies, cakes, and other goodies. Too bad those sweets were fake!

"I have some good news and some bad news," Mr. McGuire began.

Nancy, George, and Bess exchanged glances. *I wonder what the bad news is?* Nancy wondered.

"The good news is that all the costumes are now ready, thanks to Ms. Zelda's hard work," Mr. McGuire said. He smiled at Ms. Zelda, who was standing in the corner. Ms. Zelda was the costume manager. She nodded and waved.

"What's the bad news?" Deirdre asked.

Mr. McGuire's smile faded. "I just got a call from Autumn's mom," he said. "Autumn tripped on the stairs this morning and sprained her ankle. Fortunately, nothing's broken, so she's going to be fine in a couple of weeks. Unfortunately, she won't be able to dance the part of Cinderella."

Nancy gasped. Poor Autumn! She had been practicing so hard for her wonderful starring role. Now she wouldn't be able to be in the ballet at all.

"So who's going to be the new Cinderella?" a girl named Melanie asked him.

Mr. McGuire turned to Andrea, who was sitting in the back row. "Well, it only makes sense that Andrea should be the new Cinderella, since she's the understudy," he replied. Nancy remembered that an understudy was someone who learned a starring role in case he or she might have to be a substitute at the last minute.

"Yay!" Andrea squealed happily. "I mean, I feel really bad for Autumn. But I'm really glad I get to be Cinderella. And I already know all the dances!"

A boy named Rich who was sitting next to Andrea gave her a high five. Other kids congratulated her too.

Just then a pink ballet slipper came flying through the air. It hit the mirrored wall and fell to the ground.

Nancy recognized Nadine's shoe.

"That's not fair!" Nadine cried out.

ChAPTER TWO

Slippery Slippers

Nancy stared at Nadine. Mr. McGuire had just named Andrea to be the new Cinderella. And Nadine wasn't taking it very well.

Why does Nadine always have to be such a drama queen? Nancy thought.

"Ms. Nardo, we don't throw shoes in the studio!" Mr. McGuire scolded her.

"It . . . was an accident," Nadine stammered.

"Yeah, right," Bess whispered to Nancy and George. "A likely story."

"Besides, why does Andrea get to be the new Cinderella?" Nadine went on. "*I* should be the new Cinderella!"

Nadine had tried out for the part of Cinderella

last month along with Autumn and Andrea. After the audition, Mr. McGuire had picked Autumn. Afterward, he had taken a long time to choose between Andrea and Nadine to be Autumn's understudy. In the end, he had gone with Andrea and made Nadine one of the mice instead.

"Andrea is my choice and that's final," Mr. McGuire said firmly to Nadine. "Now, let's get started with the rehearsal. First we'll run through the beginning of the ballroom scene. . . ."

"Hmph," Nadine protested. She didn't say anything more.

The students scrambled to their feet and took their places. Nancy was one of the dancers at the prince's ball, along with Nadine. As the fairy godmother, Bess was not in the scene. George, playing the wicked stepmother, would not be in the scene until later.

Mr. McGuire started playing the music on the CD player. Nancy's heart began racing. The music was so elegant and regal. She could almost imagine that she was at a royal ball in a beautiful castle in some faraway kingdom. She wondered what sort of pretty ball gown she would get to wear for this scene. Would it be purple, her favorite color? Or maybe blue?

"First position," Mr. McGuire called out. All the dancers put their heels together with their toes pointed out to the sides. They held their arms curved out in front.

"*Tendu* left and *glissade* stage right," Mr. McGuire said.

Nancy had finally gotten used to hearing the ballet steps called out in French. To do the *tendu*, she slid her left foot to the side, toes pointed, knees straight. Then she slid her foot back to first position.

For the *glissade*, Nancy glided over a few feet to the right. That was one of the most confusing things about ballet. "Stage right" meant go to the right. "Stage left" meant go to the left. It had to do with the dancers' view, not the audience's view. But it sure sounded backward to Nancy.

14

Still, the *glissade* was one of Nancy's favorite steps. It felt so light and breezy, as though she was dancing on air.

"Michael, don't lock your knees. Keep them loose. Nadine, other direction," Mr. McGuire said.

"Right, left, what difference does it make," Nadine said under her breath. Nancy was dancing close to her and could hear every word. "A terrible mistake has been made!" Nadine added.

"I'm sorry you didn't get to be Cinderella," Nancy whispered to Nadine as she did a *tendu* with her right foot. "But you're an awesome dancer! We need you in this scene."

"Hmph," Nadine said.

The group continued to rehearse the steps. Nadine kept muttering about how she should have been Cinderella.

Nancy couldn't help wondering: Was Nadine going to keep complaining about not being Cinderella? Was she going to make trouble for Andrea and the other dancers?

"The Cinderella slippers have arrived!" Mr. McGuire announced.

It was Tuesday afternoon. Nancy, George, Bess, and the rest of the class were gathered in the studio for another rehearsal.

Nancy sat on the floor, pulling on her sky blue leg warmers, which matched her tights and leotard. She pulled her water bottle out of her bag and took a long drink.

"What Cinderella slippers?" Nancy asked the teacher.

"We ordered them from a very special store in Paris, France," Mr. McGuire explained. "They are for Autumn, I mean Andrea, to wear to the prince's ball. It's a lucky thing both girls wear the same shoe size. Ms. Zelda is downstairs now, getting the package from the deliveryman."

"Cinderella's glass slippers!" Bess whispered excitedly to Nancy and George.

Nancy nodded. She loved that part of the Cinderella tale.

In the story, Cinderella's fairy godmother

waved her magic wand and made Cinderella a special pair of glass slippers to wear to the prince's ball. She also turned Cinderella's raggedy dress into a beautiful ball gown, a pumpkin into a coach, and mice into coach drivers.

The fairy godmother warned Cinderella that she had to leave the ball by midnight because the magic spells would wear off then. Cinderella agreed. At the stroke of midnight, she left the prince's arms and rushed out of the ball. But in her haste, she lost one of her glass slippers. Later, the prince would comb the kingdom searching for her. He knew that whoever the tiny glass slipper fit must be his beloved princess.

"So Andrea has to dance in glass slippers?" George whispered to Nancy and Bess.

Nancy shrugged. "I don't know. She'd have to be really careful not to break them!"

Just then, Ms. Zelda came running out onto the studio floor. She was dressed in a silvery gray T-shirt and jeans. Her golden curls were piled on top of her head with fancy combs and pins. She was holding a white box covered with brightly colored stamps.

"The package has arrived from Paris!" she announced breathlessly. She had a soft voice with a French accent that sounded very sophisticated to Nancy.

"My Cinderella slippers!" Andrea exclaimed.

Mr. McGuire smiled. "Let's see them!"

Ms. Zelda started to open the box. She tried to rip the tape off. But it seemed to be stuck.

Gregory was standing next to Ms. Zelda. "You want some help, Ms. Z?" he asked her.

Ms. Zelda thrust the box at him. "*Oui*, that would be very kind."

Gregory took the box and began ripping. After a moment, he had the box open.

He reached in and pulled out a white shoe box with pink and silver stripes on it. He opened the lid and parted several layers of white tissue paper. Then he pulled out one of the glass slippers.

Nancy gasped. So did everyone else in the class. The slipper was beautiful! It was see-through and decorated with glittering, heart-shaped rhinestones. It looked very delicate.

Out of the corner of her eye, Nancy saw Deirdre get her camera out of her dance bag. She took a picture of Gregory holding the shoe.

"Deirdre, I told you before. No taking pictures during rehearsals!" Mr. McGuire called out.

Suddenly Gregory tossed the slipper in Andrea's direction.

"Catch!" he called out.

Startled, Andrea tried to catch the slipper—but missed.

Nancy gasped. Cinderella's beautiful slipper was about to hit the floor and break into a million pieces!

CHAPTER THREE

Missing!

Andrea screamed as the glass Cinderella slipper hit the hardwood floor.

But the slipper didn't break.

Gregory giggled. "What's the big deal? It's not real glass."

"Gregory!" Mr. McGuire said angrily. "Don't ever do that again!"

"What?" Gregory said innocently. "It was a joke."

"The slippers are not actually glass," Mr. McGuire explained to the rest of the class. "They're made of a certain kind of see-through plastic that looks like glass."

He glared at Gregory. "Still, never do that again. These slippers are from a very special store in Paris. If anything happened to them, we wouldn't be able to replace them in time for the show."

"Yes, Mr. McGuire," Gregory said. He hung his head sheepishly.

Andrea's face had turned ghostly white. She picked up the slipper and gave it back to Ms. Zelda. Ms. Zelda returned the shoe to the tissue-filled box. She frowned at Gregory and hurried away.

"Gregory's jokes are getting to be way too

extreme," George whispered to Nancy. Nancy nodded.

"Okay, that's enough excitement for today. Let's get started on the pumpkin coach scene," Mr. McGuire called out.

Everyone scrambled to their places, including Nancy. She closed her eyes for a moment so she could think about her part. The pumpkin scene was supertricky. On Saturday, during the real performance, she and Nadine would start the scene dressed in mice costumes. When Bess, the fairy godmother, waved her magic wand, the two girls would change into coach drivers.

In reality, Nancy and Nadine would hide behind some fake bushes for a second and slip out of their mice costumes. Underneath they would be dressed as coach drivers.

In the same scene, Andrea would change from a servant girl into a beautiful princess. Her costume switch was trickier. Nancy knew that Andrea would have to practice it lots of times before she got it just right.

"Here we go, everyone," Mr. McGuire said, clapping his hands. He turned on the CD player.

When the music began to play, Nancy pretended to be a little mouse. She curved her hands in front of her chest as though they were tiny paws. She began dancing lightly on her feet, like she was scurrying across the floor in search of cheese.

Nadine was right behind her, doing the same thing in exact time to the music. Bess was off in the corner, dancing merrily with Andrea.

Then Bess and Andrea crossed the floor with a series of graceful leaps. Just as they passed Nancy and Nadine, Nadine did a *tendu*, sticking her right foot out. Andrea tripped on Nadine's foot and fell to the floor!

"Ow!" Andrea cried out.

Mr. McGuire stopped the music. "What's going on?" he demanded.

"Nadine tripped me!" Andrea said. She sat up and brushed dust from her shorts and leotard.

"I did not!" Nadine protested. "It was an accident. I was doing my *tendu*."

"You're not supposed to do a *tendu* there, Nadine," Mr. McGuire told her sternly. "You're supposed to do a plié."

Nadine shrugged. "Oh. Sorry."

Nancy frowned. Was Nadine telling the truth? Or had she tripped Andrea on purpose?

"Smile, everyone!"

Click!

Nancy whirled around. Deirdre was standing nearby, holding her camera. She had taken a picture of Andrea, Nadine, and Mr. McGuire.

"Nadine, could you get a little closer to Andrea?" Deirdre said, gesturing with her free hand. "This will be an awesome picture for my website."

"Deirdre!" Mr. McGuire exclaimed. "I told you that I didn't want any picture taking during rehearsals. Put that camera away. In fact, you're not allowed to bring it to rehearsals anymore. It's too distracting to the other dancers."

"Oh, baloney," Deirdre said. "I mean, okay. Whatever you say, Mr. McGuire." She walked over to her dance bag.

Andrea scowled at both Nadine and Deirdre. Then she stood up and got back into position.

Suddenly Deirdre let out a scream. "Ewwww-www!" she cried out.

"Now what?" Mr. McGuire sighed.

Deirdre made a face. "Someone put Silly Putty in my camera bag!" she announced.

"Gregory!" a bunch of kids cried at once.

"Gregory!" Mr. McGuire exclaimed too.

Nancy, George, and Bess exchanged a glance. With Nadine, Gregory, and Deirdre, today's rehearsal was turning into a three-ring circus!

"I hope Nadine isn't going to trip anybody today," Bess said.

"I hope Gregory isn't going to put anything yucky in anybody's dance bag today," George added.

"I hope Deirdre isn't going to be running

around with her camera today," Nancy piped up.

It was Wednesday after school. The three girls were on their way to Mr. McGuire's studio for another rehearsal.

Wednesday! Nancy thought. That meant there were only two more regular rehearsals—today and tomorrow—before the big dress rehearsal on Friday night. During dress rehearsal, all the dancers would be wearing their costumes and makeup.

And Saturday was opening night! Nancy's father, Carson Drew, would be there along with Hannah Gruen. Hannah was the Drews' house-keeper. But she was much more than that. Hannah had helped raise Nancy since she was three years old. That's when Nancy's mother had died. George's and Bess's families would be at the opening night performance too.

The three girls finally reached Mr. McGuire's studio. They ran up the stairs, their dance bags swinging from their shoulders.

"I think we're rehearsing the ballroom scene," Nancy called out to her friends.

"I *love* that scene," Bess gushed. "It's so pretty!"

They got to the top of the stairs. Nancy expected to see all the students stretching at the barre and on the floor. But instead, everyone was huddled around Mr. McGuire. He looked very serious.

Andrea turned around and saw Nancy and her friends. She came running up to them. "Nancy! Bess! George!" she cried out. Her eyes were shiny with tears.

"Andrea, what's going on?" Nancy asked her curiously.

"My Cinderella slippers are gone," Andrea announced. "Somebody stole them!"

CHAPTER FOUR

The First Clue

"What?" Nancy exclaimed. She couldn't believe the Cinderella slippers were missing.

"Who stole them?" George asked Andrea.

"We don't know," Andrea replied. She brushed a tear from her eye. "I can't dance on Saturday night without my glass slippers! What am I going to do?"

Nancy rushed up to the crowd around Mr. McGuire. He was talking to Ms. Zelda. Andrea, Bess, and George followed.

"Where did you put them, exactly?" Mr. McGuire was asking Ms. Zelda.

Ms. Zelda pointed to the storage area in the corner of the studio. Costumes hung neatly on metal racks. Shoes, hats, and other accessories were lined up on shelves.

"I . . . I put them over there last night, in their box," Ms. Zelda said. "The box is still there. But the slippers, they are gone! I have searched the whole studio three, four times. Oh, Monsieur McGuire, what are we going to do?"

Mr. McGuire turned to the sea of faces. "Does anybody know anything about this? Gregory?"

Maybe Mr. McGuire thinks this was one of Gregory's practical jokes, Nancy thought. *If it was, it's not very funny.*

"Who, me?" Gregory exclaimed, looking surprised. "I don't know anything. Honest!"

Mr. McGuire sighed. "All right. Ms. Zelda, please send an e-mail to the store in Paris and see if there's any way we can get a replacement pair sent by overnight courier. The rest of you, five minutes of stretches, then we'll start rehearsal."

Ms. Zelda bowed her head and hurried off. The students scattered around the floor and began their stretches.

Nancy, George, and Bess found an empty spot on the floor and sat down. Andrea sat down next to them.

"Hey," Andrea said in a low voice. "The three of you have a detective club, right? The Glue Crew?"

"The Clue Crew," Bess corrected her.

"Right. The Clue Crew," Andrea said quickly. "Can I hire the Clue Crew to find the missing slippers? I'll give you all my allowance for this week."

"You don't need to pay us," Nancy replied.

"Our club is all about being the best kid detectives ever. Not about making money," George added.

"And yes, we'll take your case," Bess piped up. She glanced at Nancy and George. "Um, if that's okay with you two."

Nancy and George nodded. Nancy felt a rush of excitement. She loved solving mysteries—even more than she loved dancing.

"We'll get on the case right away," Nancy told Andrea. "We'll do our best to find the slippers by Saturday."

George was busy rehearsing a scene with Deirdre and Madison. Nancy and Bess checked all the shoe boxes and accessory boxes on the shelves one more time. The missing slippers were nowhere to be found.

"This is so mysterious," Bess said as she picked

up yet another box and peered into it. "It's like they disappeared into thin air!"

"I know what you mean," Nancy said. "But they *have* to be somewhere. Things can't just disappear into thin air."

"I guess you're right," Bess agreed. "Slippers, where are you?" she called out.

Nancy sighed. The funny thing was, the box for the slippers was still there. It was on the shelf right where Ms. Zelda had left it last night. It was a pretty white box with pink and silver stripes and writing on the side.

"There's *got* to be a clue," Bess muttered. She picked up the pink and silver striped box and turned it upside down.

Just then, Nancy noticed something odd. Gregory was walking toward the storage area with Scruffy on a leash. Scruffy had his nose low to the ground, as though he was sniffing for something.

Gregory was looking at the ground the whole time too. In fact, he didn't even seem to notice Nancy and Bess.

That Gregory acts so strange sometimes! Nancy thought.

But Nancy's thoughts were interrupted by Bess's voice.

"Nancy!" Bess exclaimed. "I found something. I think it's a clue to the missing slippers!"

"I've never seen a barrette like that," George remarked.

Nancy sat cross-legged on her bed and leaned over to take a look. George was holding a silver barrette in the palm of her hand. It was zigzag shaped.

Bess had found the barrette at the dance studio, wedged into a crack in the shelf under the pink and silver striped shoe box.

George handed the barrette to Nancy. Then she moved over to Nancy's desk and started typing on the computer. This was one of George's jobs in the Clue Crew: entering and keeping track of the case on Nancy's computer.

"Clue: Zigzaggy barrette found under the

Cinderella shoe box," George read out loud as she typed.

"Do you think the slipper thief left it there by accident?" Bess suggested.

"Or maybe the barrette was there all along and doesn't have anything to do with the slipper thief," Nancy pointed out.

George typed all this into the computer.

Nancy turned the barrette over and over

in her hand. *It looks like a* Z, she thought. She turned it over again. *Now it looks more like an* N.

N—as in Nadine?

Did the barrette belong to Nadine? Nancy wondered. *Was Nadine the slipper thief?*

ChAPTER FiVE

The Drama Queen

Nancy held the barrette out to George and Bess. "At first I thought it was a *Z* shape," she said. She turned it sideways. "But now I'm wondering if it's an *N* shape."

"Maybe," George said.

Bess nodded slowly. She seemed to be following Nancy's train of thought. "That means it could be Nadine's! She wears barrettes."

Nancy leaned back against her pile of fluffy pillows and was quiet.

"Nadine was really, really mad that Andrea got to be Cinderella instead of her," Nancy said after a while.

George nodded. "It looked like she tried to

trip Andrea yesterday at rehearsal. But it might have been an accident."

"No way," Bess said. She grabbed a handful of buttery popcorn that Hannah had made for the girls. "That was *no* accident."

"So maybe Nadine stole the slippers to ruin the 'Cinderella' ballet for Andrea and everybody else," Nancy mused. "And while she was stealing them, her barrette fell and got stuck in the crack in the shelf."

George typed everything into the computer. "Let's look at it from a different angle. What if the barrette fell and got stuck there some other time? Like last week or last month or whatever?" she said out loud.

"Or what if the barrette belongs to somebody else with the initial *N*?" Bess added.

"I think we need to talk to Nadine as soon as possible," Nancy announced.

"I have to ask you something," Nancy told Nadine.

It was Thursday, a few minutes before rehearsal. The studio was already crowded with dancers who were stretching and getting ready. Nancy, Bess, and George had found Nadine in the corner by herself.

Nadine tugged her black leg warmers over her tights and glanced up at Nancy and her friends. "What?" she asked suspiciously.

Nancy pulled the silver barrette out of her dance bag and held it out to Nadine. "Is this yours?"

Nadine stared at the barrette. "Nope, that's not mine. Lately I only wear barrettes that are shaped like flowers, animals, or musical notes. That one is shaped like . . . well, I'm not sure what it's shaped like. It's either a lightning bolt or a really skinny tree."

"Actually, we think it's the letter *N*," George piped up.

"We? What do you mean, *we*? You're not on one of your crazy Clue Crew cases, are you?" Nadine asked.

"We are. We're trying to find the missing Cinderella slippers," Bess replied. "This barrette is a clue. A very *important* clue."

Nadine's jaw dropped. "Am I one of your suspects?" she demanded.

"Where were you between the end of Tuesday's rehearsal and the beginning of Wednesday's rehearsal?" Nancy asked her.

"Did you steal the slippers?" Bess blurted out.

"What made you do it, Nadine?" George added.

"I don't believe this!" Nadine exclaimed. "Of course I didn't steal those stupid slippers. Why is everyone so worried about them, anyway? Andrea can wear another pair of ballet shoes. *I'm* the real victim here. I was rejected for the part of Cinderella, not once, but twice!" She held up two fingers and stabbed them in the air dramatically.

"Maybe you stole the slippers because you're mad about not getting the part," Bess said.

"Of course I'm mad. I should have been

Cinderella!" Nadine huffed. "But why would I make things even worse by committing a crime? I don't want to spend opening night in jail!"

Nancy, Bess, and George exchanged a look. Nadine was being her usual drama-queen self. But was she telling the truth about not stealing the slippers?

Sometimes clues are a lot easier to figure out than people, Nancy thought.

On the studio floor, rehearsal was under way for one of the Act Two scenes. Nancy watched George, Bess, and some of the other dancers practicing pirouettes with Mr. McGuire's help. Pirouettes involved spinning on one foot and were difficult to do.

Nancy was not in this scene, so she took the opportunity to do a second search for clues. This time, she crawled around on the floor on her hands and knees to get a really close look. She peeked into every crevice. She peered into every nook and cranny. She found a lot of rusty bobby pins, empty paper cups, and dust bunnies. *Yuck,* she thought, making a face.

And then she found something a little more interesting in the set storage area. It was a small piece of white paper, half hidden under a shelf. She picked it up and stared at it closely. It said, "taille 35."

Nancy frowned. What did "taille" mean? Was that code for something?

Then she noticed that the words "taille 35" were written in the same fancy cursive style as the letters on the Cinderella shoe box. *Maybe the piece of paper came from inside the shoe box*, she thought.

It's definitely a clue, Nancy told herself.

She stuffed the piece of paper in her pocket and made a mental note to discuss it with her fellow Clue Crew detectives later. Then she brushed the dust off her tights and headed over to where her dance bag lay on the floor.

On her way, she almost tripped over Gregory's legs. He was sitting on the floor, going through his own dance bag. Scruffy was sitting next to him, sniffing everything.

Gregory moved his legs out of the way. "Oh, sorry," he mumbled.

Nancy glanced down. Gregory had dumped some of the contents of his dance bag out on the floor. There were some dirty socks, a water bottle, school notebooks, homework assignments, a half-eaten granola bar, dirty T-shirts, and a dirty towel. What a mess!

"Are you cleaning out your bag?" Nancy asked him curiously.

Gregory shook his head. "Nah. Just looking for something."

"Oh."

Nancy turned to go. But just then she noticed something shiny and glittery in the pile of Gregory's stuff.

It was a rhinestone. A small, clear, heart-shaped rhinestone.

It looked just like the rhinestones from the missing Cinderella slippers!

ChaPTER Six

A Blazing Headline

Nancy stared at the glittery, heart-shaped rhinestone lying among Gregory's things. It had to have fallen off one of the Cinderella slippers.

Did this mean that Gregory was the slipper thief?

"That looks like one of the rhinestones from the Cinderella slippers," Nancy said, pointing to the jewel.

Gregory stared at the rhinestone. His cheeks flushed red.

"That's not mine," he said quickly. "I don't know how it got there."

Nancy tried to figure out if Gregory was lying.

She couldn't tell. Still, he seemed to be hiding *something.*

"You don't know how it got there?" Nancy asked him.

"No way," Gregory said.

"It's definitely not yours?" Nancy persisted.

Gregory shook his head.

Nancy picked up the rhinestone. "Can I have it, then?"

"Sure," Gregory said with a shrug. "I don't want it."

Scruffy nuzzled his nose in Nancy's hand and sniffed the rhinestone. He began barking loudly.

"What's the matter, boy?" Nancy asked him.

Scruffy continued to bark at the jewel.

"Scruffy, be quiet!" Gregory said. He picked up one of his dirty socks and threw it across the floor. "Fetch, Scruffy!" he ordered.

Just then Nancy got an idea. While Gregory watched Scruffy fetch his sock, she leaned over and peeked into his dance bag. If Gregory was the slipper thief, the slippers might be in there.

But they weren't. All she could see was a paperback book, a magazine, and . . . a magnifying glass.

A magnifying glass? Nancy frowned. What was Gregory doing with that?

Scruffy had finally stopped barking and was chewing vigorously on Gregory's sock. Nancy turned to Gregory with a smile. "So why are you carrying a magnifying glass in your dance bag?" she asked him.

Gregory started. "Hey, what are you doing looking in my bag?" he demanded.

"It was open, and I just happened to—" Nancy began.

Gregory picked up his belongings and threw them into his bag. "You should stop poking around in other people's stuff," he said gruffly.

With that, he grabbed his bag and headed over to the barre.

That night, the Clue Crew met at Nancy's house to go over their case. Nancy and Bess sat cross-legged on Nancy's bed while George sat at Nancy's desk.

"We have two new clues," Nancy announced.

She held out the heart-shaped rhinestone and the piece of paper that said, "taille 35." Bess and George studied them carefully.

"What does 'taille' mean?" Bess mused. "Did somebody misspell the word 'tail,' as in a doggy tail?"

"Maybe it's in code," George suggested.

"I wondered about that too," Nancy said. "In any case, I think it's definitely a clue because the letters are just like the fancy letters on the slipper shoe box."

George typed all this into Nancy's computer. "I know," she said suddenly. "Why don't I do a search for the word 'taille' on the Internet?"

"That's an awesome idea!" Nancy said eagerly.

George got on the Internet and typed in

a series of commands. After a moment, she glanced up from the computer. "It's a French word pronounced like 'tie,'" she announced. "It means 'size.'"

"Size?" Bess frowned. "So 'taille thirty-five' means size thirty-five?"

"I've never heard of a size thirty-five," Nancy said.

"Me neither," George said. "It sounds really, really big!"

George entered this new information into the computer. As she typed, Bess took the rhinestone from Nancy and examined it closely.

"It's so pretty," Bess said. Then she frowned. "If Gregory stole the Cinderella slippers and put them in his dance bag, the rhinestone could have fallen off one of the slippers."

"Or someone could have planted the rhinestone there to make him look guilty," Nancy pointed out.

George looked up from the computer. "We have three clues now: the barrette, the piece of paper with 'taille 35,' or size 35, on it, and the rhinestone heart," she reminded the other members of the Clue Crew. "The barrette doesn't exactly fit with Gregory being the thief."

"That's true," Nancy agreed. "Although Gregory sure owns a lot of weird stuff. Today I saw a magnifying glass in his dance bag."

"A magnifying glass?" Bess repeated. "Who does he think he is, Sherlock Holmes?"

Just then, a bell-like *ting!* sounded on Nancy's computer. George peered at the screen. "Andrea is instant messaging us," she announced.

"What did she say?" Nancy asked, leaning over.

"She says, 'Check out Deirdre's website right away,'" George read.

"Deirdre's website?" Bess repeated, looking confused.

George typed in the address for the Dishing with Deirdre site. Nancy and Bess got up from the bed and gathered around George.

The home page of Dishing with Deirdre filled

Nancy's computer screen. Across the top of it was the blazing headline WHO STOLE CINDERELLA'S SHOES?

"What!" Bess burst out.

"Typical Deirdre," George muttered.

Nancy reached forward for the mouse and used it to scroll down the page. Deirdre had written a "late-breaking story" about the theft of the Cinderella slippers from Tim McGuire's dance studio.

Then Nancy noticed something strange. Deirdre had included a photograph of the Cinderella slippers.

The slippers were lined up on a sidewalk in front of a brick wall.

What is wrong with this picture? Nancy asked herself.

ChaPTeR SeVeN

A New Suspect

Nancy pointed to the photo. "Do you notice something really weird?" she asked her friends.

George and Bess stared at the photo. "N-no," George said after a moment.

"It's just a picture of the slippers," Bess said, shrugging.

Nancy stabbed her finger at the computer screen. "This photo was taken *outside*," she explained. "How did Deirdre take a photo of the slippers outside?"

Bess gasped. "She must have taken the slippers from the studio!" she exclaimed.

George's eyes widened. "Maybe Deirdre is the slipper thief!" she said.

Nancy peered at the screen. "George, can you make this photo bigger?" she asked.

"No problem," George said.

George's fingers flew over the keyboard as she zoomed the photo to 150 percent, then 200 percent. "Is that big enough for you?" she asked Nancy.

Nancy nodded. "Perfect! Now, can you print it out?"

George went into the print menu and hit several keys. Nancy's printer whirred to life. A minute later it spit out a color copy of Deirdre's photo. The copy was twice the original size of the photo.

Nancy studied the printout. "None of the heart-shaped rhinestones are missing," she said after a moment. "That means this photo was taken *before* the rhinestone got into Gregory's bag somehow."

"Maybe Deirdre stole the slippers, then planted the rhinestone in Gregory's bag to make him look guilty," Bess suggested.

"Maybe," Nancy agreed.

"Deirdre's photo is an important clue," George said. "I have a feeling the Clue Crew is getting close to solving the case!"

"Yes!" Bess said, giving George a high five.

"I hope you guys are right," Nancy told her friends.

On Friday during recess, Nancy, George, and Bess found Deirdre on the swings. Madison was pushing her. The day was cool but sunny. A slight breeze stirred the leaves on the trees.

"Higher, higher!" Deirdre shouted to Madison.

Madison pushed Deirdre extra hard. Then she caught sight of Nancy and her friends and stopped.

"Madison, push!" Deirdre shouted.

"Uh, Deirdre? We've got company," Madison said.

Deirdre glanced down. She frowned when she saw Nancy and the others.

"Oh," Deirdre muttered. *You* guys."

"Hello to you, too!" Bess called out cheerfully.

Deirdre dug her shoes into the dirt to slow down the swing. Dust sprayed up into the air. The swing came to a stop.

"Did you see the late-breaking story on my website?" Deirdre asked the girls with a sly smile.

"We sure did," Bess replied.

"It was a really interesting read," George added.

"And you had a really interesting photo to go with it," Nancy piped up.

Deirdre beamed. "Thanks! I took it myself, of course."

Nancy smiled. "Of course. Right *after* you took the slippers from Mr. McGuire's studio."

"More like *stole*," Bess said meaningfully.

"What made you do it, Deirdre?" George asked her.

Deirdre's cheeks flushed red. "What are you talking about? I'm not the slipper thief! I just took a photo, that's all," she insisted.

"Deirdre's totally innocent," Madison defended her friend. Nancy noticed that Madison kept her eyes on the ground, though. *Is she hiding something?* Nancy wondered.

"I think you guys are taking this Clue Crew stuff a little too seriously," Deirdre said, her tone turning mean. "I mean, it's not like you're real detectives or anything."

Nancy dug into her pocket and pulled out the folded-up computer printout. She unfolded it and held it up for Deirdre to see.

"Well, this is a *real* clue," Nancy said coolly.

"And according to this clue, you took this photo outside. Which means that you took the slippers from the studio."

Madison gasped. "Deirdre, we didn't think of that," she said, sounding panicked.

"Be quiet, Madison," Deirdre whispered.

"So you *are* the slipper thief," Nancy said to Deirdre. "Maybe you stole the slippers just so you could write a killer story about it for your website!"

Deirdre got up from the swing. She had a determined look on her face. "I am absolutely, definitely not the slipper thief," she said firmly. "All I did was . . . well, I kind of *borrowed* the slippers for, like, one or two seconds on Tuesday."

"What does that mean, 'borrowed'?" Bess asked her.

"I wanted to take a photo of the slippers for my website because they were so awesome looking and special," Deirdre explained. "But Mr. McGuire said I couldn't take photos in his studio because it bothered the other dancers or whatever. So I borrowed the slippers during a break. I took them outside, took the photo, and then brought them right back in. It was Madison's idea," she added.

"We didn't steal the slippers," Madison insisted.

"I thought Mr. McGuire said that you couldn't even bring your camera to rehearsals any longer," George said to Deirdre.

"He doesn't understand," Deirdre complained. "A reporter can't be without her camera!"

Nancy was thoughtful. "You took the photo on Tuesday," she said after a moment. "But you didn't post your story until Wednesday, after the slippers were missing. "

Deirdre nodded. "The whole thing was kind of a coincidence. I took the photo on Tuesday and posted it on my website Tuesday night. Ask anybody! Then on Wednesday, we all found out at rehearsal that the slippers had been stolen. When I got home that night, I wrote my excellent piece called, 'Who Stole Cinderella's Shoes?'

I posted it right away, next to the photo. I was really glad that I just happened to have the photo to go with the story."

Nancy considered this. Deirdre sounded like she was telling the truth. Or was she?

The bell rang, signaling the end of recess. "Gotta go," Deirdre said, waving at Nancy and the girls. "Good luck with your Crew Clue or whatever."

"Clue Crew!" George corrected her.

Deirdre ignored George. She turned and hurried through a crowd of kids toward the door. Madison followed close behind.

"Do we believe her?" Bess asked Nancy and George.

"I don't know," George replied, frowning in Deirdre's direction.

Nancy stuffed the printout of Deirdre's photo back into her pocket. "I don't know either," she said worriedly. "But I *do* know this: Tomorrow is opening night. We're running out of time!"

CHAPTER EIGHT

The French Clue

"It's the dress rehearsal, and I don't have any shoes to wear!" Andrea said, her eyes welling with tears.

It was Friday night. Mr. McGuire's studio was filled with the cast of the "Cinderella" ballet. Parents and other volunteers were busy helping the children on with their costumes or stage makeup.

"You can wear your pink ballet slippers for tonight," Mr. McGuire told Andrea. His cell phone began ringing. "Excuse me," he said, walking away to take the call.

Nancy was standing nearby, her mouse costume slung over her arm. She walked over to

Andrea. "It's going to be okay," she told Andrea. "The Clue Crew is going to keep looking for your Cinderella slippers until we find them!"

"I don't know," Andrea said doubtfully.

Nancy patted her dance bag. "We have those three clues I e-mailed you about: the rhinestone, the barrette, and the piece of paper with a French word on it. They're in my bag. We have some suspects, too. Don't worry, we'll find your slippers by tomorrow night."

"Okay," Andrea said. But she didn't look very sure.

One of the parents called Andrea over so she could style her hair. Andrea waved to Nancy and rushed off.

Nancy glanced around the room. Bess was getting sparkly eye shadow put on her eyelids by one of the volunteers. She looked so pretty in her fairy godmother costume, which was a glittery gold dress with a matching tiara.

George was on the other side of the studio, wearing her wicked stepmother costume: a long, dark gray dress with a high collar. Her eyebrows had been transformed into pointy, severe arches with a black eye pencil. Nancy thought George looked pretty scary!

"Can I help you on with your costume, Mademoiselle Nancy?"

Nancy turned around. Ms. Zelda was standing there. She had a box of safety pins in one hand and a sewing kit in the other. There was a long white tape measure draped around her neck.

"Thanks, Ms. Zelda, that would be great," Nancy said. Her mouse costume *was* kind of complicated.

Ms. Zelda led Nancy to a quiet corner of the studio. She took the mouse costume from Nancy and studied it carefully. "Why don't you sit on the floor and we can slip this on your feet first?" she suggested.

Nancy obeyed. Ms. Zelda tugged the mouse costume over Nancy's feet, which were covered with pink ballet tights.

"Hmm, maybe the mouse legs are still a little long," Ms. Zelda fretted. "I must pin them for you."

"Okay," Nancy said. "Thanks, Ms. Zelda."

As Ms. Zelda worked, Nancy looked around restlessly. She wished she could gather her Clue Crew around her and get back to work: searching for clues, interviewing witnesses, anything. But she knew this was dress rehearsal time. No matter how important it was to find the missing slippers, she, George, and Bess had to focus on their last chance to rehearse.

Ms. Zelda gave a big yawn. "Oh, *pardonnez-moi*," she said, covering her mouth.

"Are you sleepy?" Nancy asked with a smile.

Ms. Zelda yawned again and nodded. "I have been working so hard here lately," she explained. "Sewing all the costumes, helping with the ticket sales, even designing the program. Oh, and a few nights ago Mr. McGuire asked me to help him move some old *Nutcracker* set pieces from the set storage area up to the attic, to make room. It was hard work—*tres difficile*. My muscles still ache from that."

Nancy sat up a little straighter. The set storage area? That was where she had found the piece of paper with the words "taille 35" on it.

Nancy reached over to get her dance bag. "Don't move," Ms. Zelda instructed her. "I must put one last pin in—there! Now you can move."

Nancy opened her dance bag and pulled out the "taille" clue. She showed it to Ms. Zelda.

"Do you know what this is?" Nancy asked her.

Ms. Zelda shrugged. "*Mais oui*, of course. It is a French shoe size."

"A shoe size? Isn't thirty-five kind of big for a shoe size? Maybe it's a shoe size for giants!" Nancy giggled at her own joke.

Ms. Zelda chuckled. "No, no. France is part of Europe. European shoe sizes are different. A European size thirty-five is about—oh, let us see, a size four for girls in America."

"Really?" Nancy exclaimed.

"Yes, really." Ms. Zelda looked amused. "Now, please stand up so I can check the rest of your costume."

Nancy got to her feet. Her mind was spinning.

If taille 35 was the same as a girl's size 4, the piece of paper must have definitely fallen out of the box containing the Cinderella slippers. She remembered Andrea telling her once that she was a size 4.

Ms. Zelda bent over low to adjust Nancy's hemline. Just then Nancy noticed something. Ms. Zelda was wearing a shirt with the monogram Z embroidered on it in black.

Nancy cocked her head to the right. Sideways, the letter Z turned into the letter N. Could the silver barrette—one of the Clue Crew's clues—be a Z shape instead of an N shape, after all?

Nancy gave a little cough. "Um, excuse me, Ms. Zelda," she began. "Do you own a silver barrette?"

Ms. Zelda looked surprised. "*Oui!* But I seem to have lost it. I haven't seen it in several days."

She stared at Nancy. "Why do you ask?"

Nancy thought quickly. "I think I heard one of the other kids saying they saw something like that," she said. She wanted to hang on to her clue until she'd solved the case. "I'll ask around about it."

"Thank you, that's kind," Ms. Zelda said.

"Ms. Zelda, can you help me with my cape?" one of the other students called out. "It's too long!"

"Yes, yes, I'm coming," Ms. Zelda replied. She patted Nancy's costume, beaming. "There. You look just like a little mouse."

Nancy thanked Ms. Zelda as the older woman hurried away with her tape measure, safety pins, and sewing kit. Nancy gazed after her, wondering if the costume manager might be the slipper thief. But that didn't make any sense. Why would Ms. Zelda have stolen the slippers? Besides, Nancy didn't feel comfortable accusing her of being a thief. She was a grown-up, after all. Maybe Ms. Zelda lost the barrette, just as she said.

"Hey, Nancy Clue," someone said.

Nancy glanced up. Gregory was standing nearby. He looked handsome in his prince costume: black velvet pants and a royal white tunic with gold buttons.

"Hi, Gregory," Nancy said. She wondered if he had been eavesdropping on her conversation with Ms. Zelda.

Gregory pointed to the "taille 35" clue, which Nancy was still holding. "Where'd you get that?" he asked her curiously.

"In the set storage area," Nancy replied. "Why?"

"I want to show it to someone," Gregory said. "I'll bring it right back. Is that okay? I'll be supercareful with it."

Nancy thought for a moment. She wondered why Gregory *really* wanted to borrow the "taille 35" paper. Still, some instinct told her to say yes. Maybe she would learn something new and important about the case. After all, Gregory *was* a suspect.

"Sure," Nancy said with a smile. She handed the piece of paper to him.

"Thanks a lot!" Gregory said. Then he rushed off.

Nancy watched him as he hurried to the other side of the studio. She followed tentatively. Bess and George came up to her.

"You look so cool in your mouse clothes!" Bess exclaimed.

"You guys look really great in your costumes too," Nancy said. She lowered her voice. "I'm following Gregory."

"Why?" George asked.

Nancy explained. "I want to know what he's going to do with the 'size thirty-five' clue," she finished.

"We're all dressed and we have our makeup on," Bess whispered. "We have about twenty minutes until the first scene. We can help you!"

Nancy nodded. She put her finger to her lips. Then she, George, and Bess began following Gregory again.

The studio was bustling with activity, so Gregory didn't seem to notice that he was being watched. He walked toward Scruffy, who was curled up in the corner on an old red blanket.

Gregory bent down next to Scruffy and held the piece of paper Nancy had given him under the dog's nose. Scruffy sniffed. Gregory said something to him. Then Scruffy got up and began walking this way and that, his nose low to the ground, continuing to sniff.

"What is Gregory doing?" George whispered to Nancy.

"What is *Scruffy* doing?" Bess added.

Nancy frowned. *What* are *they doing?* she wondered.

Then something occurred to her.

"On Wednesday I saw Gregory walking around the set storage area with Scruffy," Nancy said out loud to her friends. "It's like he was using Scruffy to help him find something. Then yesterday, when I found the rhinestone in Gregory's stuff, Scruffy started sniffing it and barking like crazy."

Bess and George both stared at her. "What do you think all that means?" George asked her.

Nancy's eyes flashed. "I think I know what happened to the Cinderella slippers," she announced.

ChaPTeR NiNe

Bravo!

George gasped. "You know what happened to the slippers?" she demanded. "What? Who? Where? How? Why?"

"I think Gregory is the person who should be answering those questions," Nancy said.

Nancy marched up to Gregory and Scruffy, with George and Bess at her heels. Gregory stopped and turned around. Scruffy gave a short bark.

Nancy put her hands on her hips and stared sternly at Gregory. She felt a little silly doing that in her mouse costume. But this was important.

"You took the Cinderella slippers, didn't you?" Nancy accused Gregory.

Gregory's cheeks turned bright red. "Uh, n-no way," he stammered. "I d-don't know what you're talking about."

Bess stepped up. She put her hands on her hips too. "You *do* know," she said. "And you'd better tell us!"

Gregory stared at the floor. Scruffy barked at him.

"I think you took the Cinderella slippers on Tuesday, as a joke," Nancy guessed. "You hid them somewhere, maybe in the set storage area. Then you forgot where you hid them. Or someone moved them. Either way, now you don't know where they are. You've been looking for them since Wednesday, using Scruffy's superduper doggy nose."

Bess seemed to pick up on Nancy's thoughts. "You let Scruffy smell the rhinestone and the piece of paper with the size on it to help track down the slippers," she said slowly.

Gregory looked up and stared at her, his eyes wide. "How'd you guys know all that?" he asked her.

"That's why we're the Clue Crew," George said with a grin.

"Oh." Gregory frowned. "I didn't mean to steal the slippers, exactly," he confessed finally. "I was just going to hide them, as a joke, like

Nancy said. I did it after rehearsal on Tuesday."

"Is that the last time you saw them?" Nancy asked him.

Gregory nodded. "On Wednesday, when Andrea and everyone else figured out the slippers were missing, they all freaked out! I thought that was kind of funny. Then I went over to the hiding place to get them. But they were gone!"

"Where did you get the rhinestone?" Bess said.

"It fell off on Tuesday when I hid the slippers," Gregory replied. "I was going to glue it on later. I let Scruffy smell it so he'd help me find the slippers. He has an awesome sense of smell. I think his great-grandfather was a bloodhound."

Then something else occurred to Nancy. "That's why there was a magnifying glass in your dance bag," she said suddenly.

"Yeah. I was trying to act like a real detective so I'd solve the mystery," Gregory admitted. "I guess it didn't work. The slippers are still gone. Mr. McGuire is going to be supermad at me." He sighed unhappily.

Nancy thought for a moment. "Where did you hide the slippers on Tuesday?" she asked him.

"In a giant ice-cream sundae," Gregory replied.

"A giant ice-cream sundae?" Nancy, George, and Bess repeated in unison.

Gregory nodded. "Yeah. It was made of painted wood. It had a little shelf on the back part of it. I put the slippers there. But then the whole thing disappeared! Like, how did *that* happen?"

Nancy gasped. It all made sense now.

"I know where the sundae is!" she exclaimed.

"You do?" Gregory asked her eagerly. "Where? I'll give you my magnifying glass if you find the sundae," he offered.

"You can keep your magnifying glass," Nancy told him. "Come on, guys, we have to get up to the attic!"

"The attic?" Bess said, sounding confused.

"The giant ice-cream sundae is from *The Nut-cracker*," Nancy said, heading for the stairs.

Bess, George, and Gregory followed Nancy. The four of them raced up the stairs to the attic. Scruffy bounded behind them.

Nancy had never been in the attic before. It was a big room with a ceiling that sloped down on either side, following the lines of the roof. It was full of set pieces and props: giant trees, the fronts of buildings, fake lampposts, Victorian furniture. Everything was covered with a fine layer of dust. Scruffy sneezed; so did Bess and George.

"Okay, what's this about *The Nutcracker*?" George asked Nancy as she sneezed again.

"Ms. Zelda told me that she moved some old set pieces from *The Nutcracker* from the studio up to the attic, to make room," Nancy explained breathlessly. "This was Tuesday night. "

"Tuesday night?" Gregory cried out. "That's right after I hid the slippers."

Nancy nodded. "Exactly! Now, we just have to find the giant ice-cream sundae somehow. There's an awful lot of stuff here."

"And we can't mess up our costumes, or Mr. McGuire will *really* be mad," George pointed out.

"And we don't have a lot of time," Bess said.

But it took Nancy and her Clue Crew only a few minutes to find the giant ice-cream sundae. It had been shoved in between a huge cookie and an enormous piece of pie.

Nancy peered behind the sundae. She saw the shelf Gregory had mentioned. Actually, it was more like a little nook.

The Cinderella slippers were there!

Nancy pulled them out and held them up in the air. "Yay, we found them!" she exclaimed.

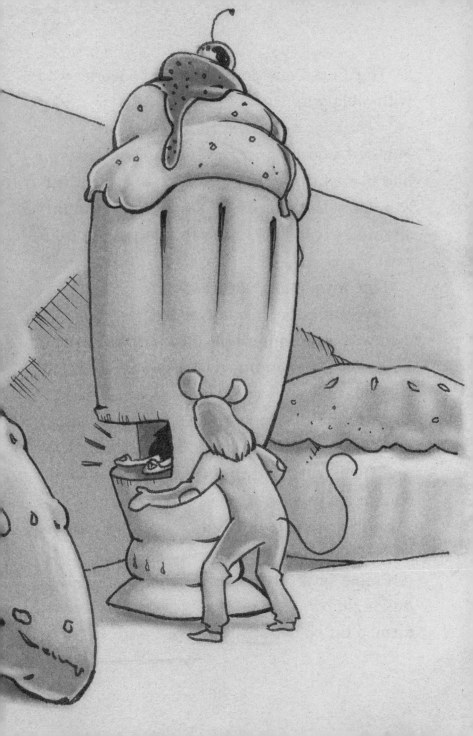

"The Clue Crew does it again," George said with a big grin.

Nancy stood behind the blue velvet curtain. She peered through a crack between two curtain panels. "Oh, I see Dad and Hannah," she said excitedly. "They're sitting in the front row!"

"I see my parents," Bess said.

"I see mine, too," George added.

It was opening night. The curtain would go up in a few minutes. Backstage, everyone was buzzing with excitement. Ms. Zelda hurried around making sure everyone's costumes were on just right. Mr. McGuire rushed here and there, checking that the lights and sound equipment were working properly.

Andrea came up to Nancy and her friends. She was dressed in her Act I Cinderella clothes: a simple gray dress, black tights, and black ballet slippers. In Act II, she would be transformed into a beautiful princess with her long pink ball gown—and of course, her special Cinderella slippers.

Andrea gave each of the three girls a big hug. "I don't know how to thank you guys," she said happily. "You really *are* the most awesome detectives in the world!"

"I'm just glad we found your slippers in time for opening night," Nancy said.

"Gregory apologized to me and Mr. McGuire," Andrea said. "He brought us both homemade cookies from his mom too. They were real this time." She giggled.

"That's good." Nancy giggled too.

"Places, everybody!" Mr. McGuire announced in a loud whisper. "Curtain in two minutes."

"Oh, my gosh!" Bess exclaimed.

Nancy and her friends ran to their places. Nancy's heart was pounding so hard that she thought it would burst out of her chest. It was opening night! And she was in the show! She was not just a real detective but a real ballerina, too.

The lights in the theater dimmed. The music began to play.

The blue velvet curtain closed after the final act. Applause rang out in the auditorium.

Behind the curtain, the dancers rushed around, looking for their places to take a bow. Nancy bumped into George.

"Ow, sorry!" Nancy giggled.

"Wasn't that awesome?" George said breathlessly.

Bess ran up to them. "That was so much fun," she said. "I think we should all be dancers when we grow up!"

"Dancer-detectives," George said, nodding. "We'll solve mysteries during the day and dance on stage at night!"

Mr. McGuire stepped out from one of the stage wings. His usually serious-looking face was glowing with excitement. "Places, everyone!" he said in a loud whisper. "It's time to take your bows."

"I can't believe it's over!" Bess gasped.

Nancy took her place. So did George, Bess, and the other dancers. After a few seconds, the curtain swished open. Nancy was dazzled. Her eyes took a minute to focus because the stage lights were so bright, and the auditorium was dark.

Everyone was clapping like mad. Nancy tried to make out her father and Hannah in the audience. She finally spotted them. Her father was holding a bouquet of flowers and a big stuffed teddy bear. They were for Nancy!

Then Mr. Drew and the whole audience stood up. This was a standing ovation, which meant that the people really, really liked the ballet.

Nancy took her bow along with the other dancers. After a moment, Andrea swept out from the wing of the stage and took a special bow, since she was Cinderella. The crowd clapped even more loudly. Andrea looked so pretty. Her Cinderella slippers glittered brightly under the stage lights.

The curtain closed, then opened again. The audience just kept clapping. Nancy turned to look at George and Bess and grinned. They grinned back.

The Clue Crew had done it again!

Nancy, Bess, and George's Ballerina Finger Puppets

Nancy, Bess, and George love to put on a show of their own with these cute ballerina finger puppets. You can too!

You will need:

White posterboard
Pencil
Scissors
Markers
Construction paper or
   wrapping paper
Glue
Fabric scraps
Colored (not clear) fingernail polish
Glitter, small rhinestones (optional)

*Draw the outline of a ballerina on the poster-board with the pencil. Just draw the ballerina's head, torso, and arms—no legs. Her head and torso together should be about as tall as the length of your hand from your wrist to your knuckles. Her arms can be posed like ballerina arms—out to the side, over her head, or one arm up and one arm to the side. You decide!

*Cut out your ballerina shape with the scissors. Near the bottom of the torso, cut out two legholes for your fingers to go through. (Your fingers will be the ballerina's legs!)

*Use the markers to draw her eyes, nose, and mouth. You can make her smiling or serious—or even mean-looking, like Cinderella's wicked stepmother!

*Use the construction paper or wrapping paper to create her hair and leotard. Sketch the hair and leotard with the pencil, then cut them out with scissors, and glue them onto your posterboard ballerina. Another option: You can use markers to draw her hair and leotard instead.

*Use the fabric scraps to create her tutu (which is a fancy French word for a ballet skirt). Cut a triangle shape that would be the right size for a skirt; then trim one corner of the triangle so it can be her waist. Glue the tutu onto your posterboard ballerina.

*If you want, you can glue glitter or small rhinestones onto her leotard or tutu (or even her hair).

*Paint the fingernails of your middle finger and the finger next to your thumb with a pretty color. Those will be your ballerina's toe shoes! When your fingernails are dry, put those fingers through the two legholes in your ballerina's torso.

It's Time to Dance!

Drape a pretty scarf or other cloth over a table, the back of a chair, or other hard surface for your ballerina's "stage." Then put on a CD of classical music like *The Nutcracker* by Tchaikovsky or *A Midsummer Night's Dream* by Mendelssohn—or whatever music you and your ballerina feel like grooving to.

The More the Merrier

Invite your friends over to make ballerina finger puppets with you. Then you can all put on a show together! If you want to make finger puppets from the Cinderella ballet, you can use these instructions to make a fancy Cinderella, a fairy godmother, or even mice!

How Did They Do Leaps and Jumps in THAT?

In the early days of ballet, dancers' skirts came all the way down to the floor. But eventually, dancers wanted costumes that would show off their steps and make it easier for them to move around. In the early 1700s, dancers started wearing ballet skirts above their ankles. Over the next three hundred years, the ballet skirts continued to get shorter and shorter.